ISBN 978-1-989025-05-5 (hardback)   ISBN 978-1-989025-19-2 (ebook)

Produced by Page Two Books www.pagetwobooks.com
Book art direction and design by Elisa Gutiérrez
Illustrations by Ipek Konak
Editing by Kallie George
With writing support from Betsy Beyer and Isaac Andres
Art direction support from Amy Yip
Creative vision of Komal Singh

Printed and bound in Canada by Friesens
Distributed in Canada by Raincoast Books
Distributed in the US and internationally by Publishers Group West
All profits from sales of the book will go to STEM-related charities or non-profits.

18 19 20 21 22   5 4 3 2 1

This book is not an official product of Google.
Publication of this book has been undertaken by Google employees in their personal capacity.

www.arastarengineer.com

Ara
the Star Engineer

by Komal Singh
and other **thinkers** and **tinkerers** at Google

illustrations by
Ipek Konak

PAGE TWO
BOOKS

For A, who loves infinity and one-quarter.

For baby Z, who hung in there with me, quite literally.—KS

Dear parents and mentors,

I'm a techie by day and a storyteller mom by night—someone who loves coding and cupcakes, data crunching and daydreaming. The idea for this book was born when my daughter proclaimed, at age four, "Engineers are boys." This left me stunned.

Having plotted my own journey as a woman in tech, this revalidated for me that representation is imperative. Research shows girls start doubting their STEM intelligence (science, technology, engineering and mathematics) by the time they are six years old. The innocuous repartee I often hear is, "Well, it's because girls are simply not interested in STEM functions." But that's not true. Most girls aren't provided an opportunity to be interested in STEM in the first place. Storybooks and media offer a marginal spotlight on women role models for young girls to relate to and aspire to be. This, combined with our unconscious biases, tends to make girls believe excelling in STEM is an *innate ability* rather than an *acquired quality.* Yet, some of the very first pioneers in computer science have been women. Only when PCs were marketed in the 1980s as toys for boys and men did we start seeing a massive drop in the number of women in computer science.

I hope you will use this book as a tool to relevel STEM playing fields. To inspire beautiful minds of all genders, young and old. To meet women engineer trailblazers of diverse color and background who are solving some of the biggest problems in computing today! This story introduces computer science concepts in a playful manner that can be further explored through learning resources in the accompanying notebook and the book website, www.arastarengineer.com.

Read together, learn, wonder—and stop and gawk at the data center.

Komal Singh

Hello, World!

I am Ara.

This is my assistant, DeeDee.

We both love to learn about BIG numbers.
Did you know there is a number with one hundred
zeros in it? It's called **googol**. *Googol* was named by
a nine-year-old kid!

Did you know that my name, Ara, is also the name of a constellation with seven stars?

But there are WAY more than seven stars out there.

I wonder how many—a zillion, a gazillion, a *googol*?

Let's find out!

To count such a big number of stars very fast, I'll need the help of a computer.

"Like you, DeeDee! How do I program you to count stars?"

Beep!

MY FIRST HOME

Oh! Of course! DeeDee was invented by engineer superheroes at *Innovation Plex*. I bet they would love to help us!

"Okay, DeeDee—let's go to the *Plex*!"

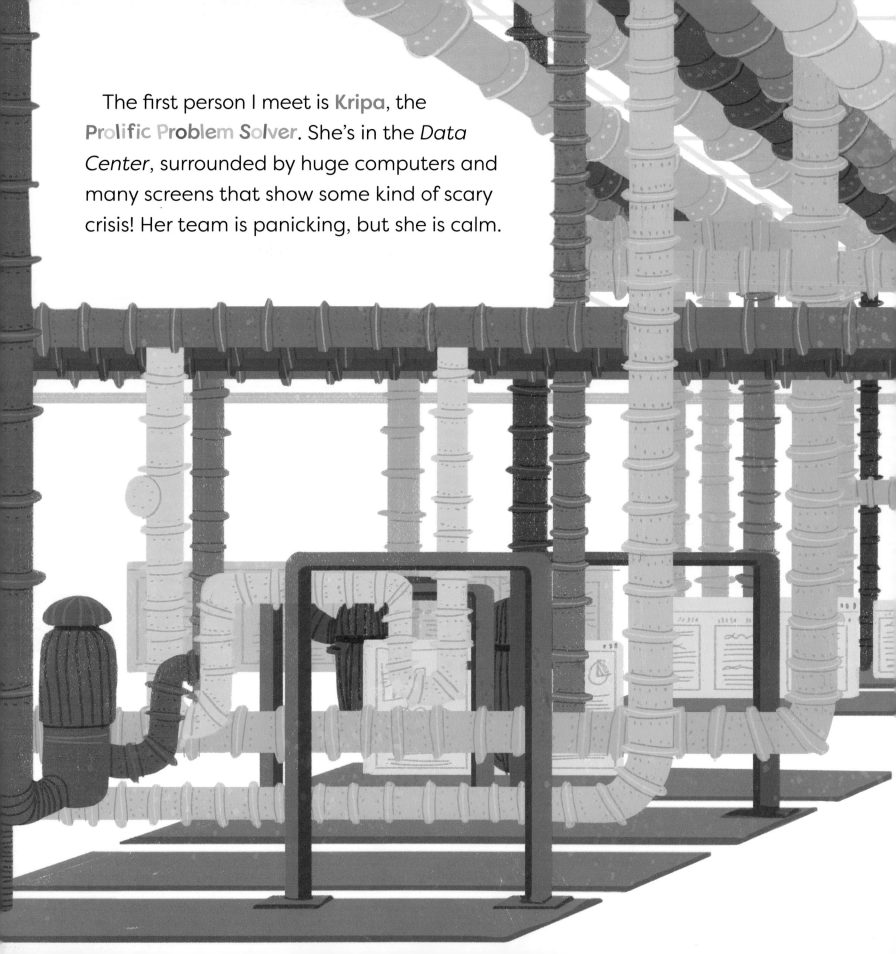

The first person I meet is **Kripa**, the *Prolific Problem Solver*. She's in the *Data Center*, surrounded by huge computers and many screens that show some kind of scary crisis! Her team is panicking, but she is calm.

"How do you figure out the problem and keep thousands of computers running?" I ask.

"Let's analyze!" says Kripa. "Any big problem can be solved with a **plan**. Each of these screens gives us a peek into the larger problem . . .

. . . you look at each screen one at a time . . .

. . . and you work on one small part of the problem at a time.

The big problem is solved and doesn't seem so scary anymore!"

"Aha!"

"I get it. I can come up with my own plan! I can break down the big problem of counting so many stars by galaxies, and count them one galaxy at a time!"

courage

"I admire your **courage**, Ara, to solve such a big problem," says Kripa. "Good luck!"

Beep!

Next we meet Parisa, the Intrepid Innovator.
She's in the *Ideas Lab*, pondering big problems.

"What makes you an innovator?"
I quiz her excitedly.

IDEAS LAB

Parisa smiles. "I create new solutions that make computers solve big problems."

"Great! I have a plan for counting stars, but I still have so many questions."

"Let's brainstorm!" says Parisa. "You can start by writing an algorithm."

"**Algorithm**?" That's a BIG word.

Parisa hands me a cupcake. "It's just a fancy name for a recipe. Like a recipe, an algorithm is a set of step-by-step instructions to get something done."

We brainstorm together and come up
with a recipe—an algorithm—for my plan.

"Aha!"

<My Algorithm>
Step 1: Okay DeeDee, first count all the
stars in my favorite galaxy 'MilkyWay'
Step 2: Repeat
Step 2.1 If there is another galaxy
Step 2.1.1 Count stars in the
new galaxy
Step 2.1.2 Go to Step 2
Step 2.2 Else, go to Step 3
Step 3: Okay DeeDee, stop counting!
</My Algorithm>

creativity

"I'm impressed by your **creativity**, Ara, in creating an algorithm all on your own!" says Parisa.

Beep!

"But how will DeeDee understand a brand-new algorithm? DeeDee has only been programmed to do easy tasks."

Parisa smiles. "For that, you need to turn your algorithm into code."

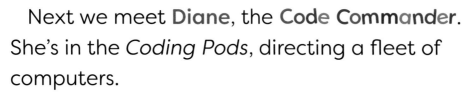

Next we meet **Diane**, the **Code Commander**.
She's in the *Coding Pods*, directing a fleet of
computers.

"Can you actually command computers?"
I ask her curiously.

"I sure can," Diane says, "by writing **code**. Just as people speak and write in different languages, we use coding languages to communicate with computers."

"That's what I need to do," I say. "I have an algorithm, and now I need to code it."

"Let's program!" says Diane.

We jump into coding basics. It's tricky but fun.

"Aha!"

```
<My Code>
DeeDee.countStars ("MilkyWay");
Loop
   If DeeDee.moreGalaxiesExist()
      DeeDee.countStars (new galaxy);
   else
      DeeDee.stop();
</MyCode>
```

At last we have robust code to communicate my algorithm to DeeDee.

YUMMY CODE!

code

"I love your eagerness to **code**, Ara!" says Diane. "This gives you the power to **communicate** with any computer." I feel proud. "And now I am ready to count the stars!"

Beep!

"Okay, DeeDee—let's launch!
Ready, set, go."
DeeDee starts to count . . .

Beep!

100
000

displays a number . . .

Beep!

Beep. . .

. . . but STOPS!

"Oh no, DeeDee has an error."

I slump down. I'm so disappointed.

"Engineering something new is so tough,"
I say to DeeDee. "I don't think I can do it."

"You're right, DeeDee.

I'm a problem solver. I won't give up!"

So we go to meet Marian, the Tenacious Troubleshooter.
She's in the *X-Space*, designing and fixing all sorts of machines.

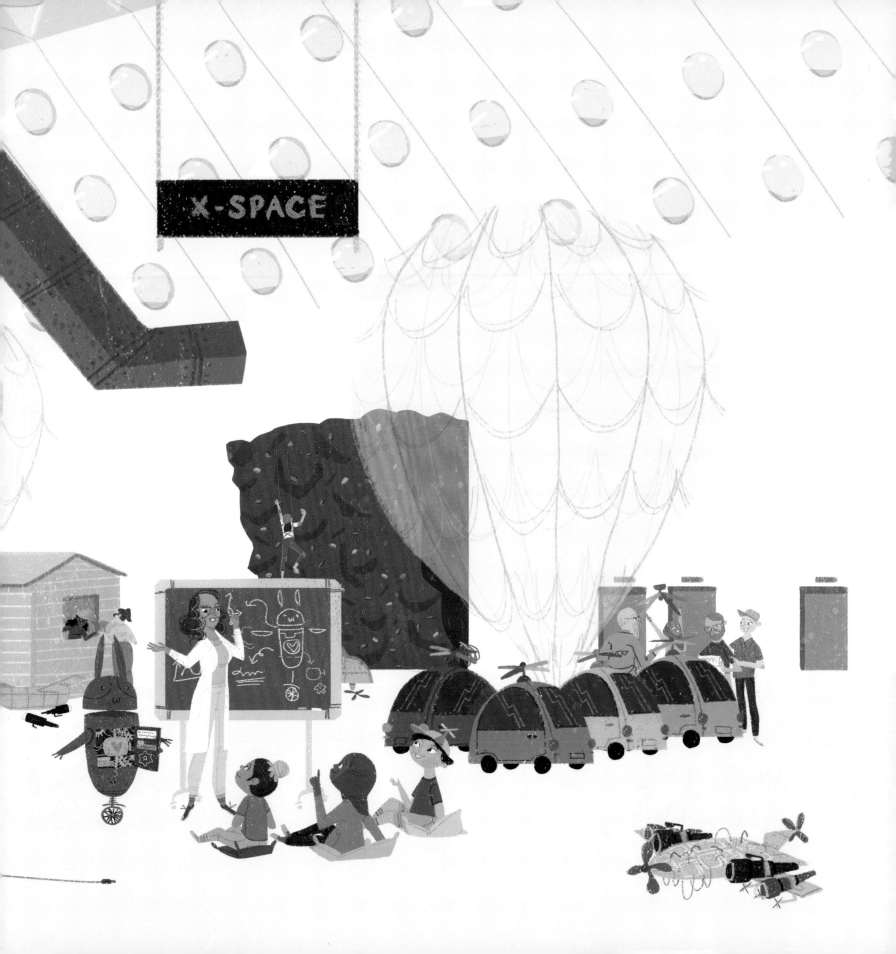

"DeeDee has an error and can't count enough stars. Can you help us?" I ask her hopefully.

"Absolutely, " answers Marian. "Let's improve DeeDee!"

She takes a closer look.

"Hmmm . . . it looks like DeeDee needs more **computing power**." She hands me a processor and a memory chip.

. . . more processors . . .
. . . more memory . . .
. . . more storage . . .

TROUBLE-
SHOOTING
. . .

Together, we successfully troubleshoot DeeDee.

collaboration

"I really like your spirit of **collaboration**, Ara," Marian proclaims. "Working as a team with so many engineers has helped you fix problems faster!"

"Okay, DeeDee—let's launch version two . . ."

Beep!

SHOW TIME!

We are now ready to count the stars.
"Ready, set, go!"

WHOA, what a huge number of stars . . .
even more than a googol!

Success!

Just as all the engineers cheer us, I share
another discovery with everyone:
"I know an amazing algorithm to solve
any problem:

courage, creativity, code and collaboration!

Right, DeeDee?"

KRIPA KRISHNAN
PROLIFIC PROBLEM SOLVER

KRIPA is a Senior Director of Technical Program Management at Google. She is known as the *Queen of Chaos* because she led a team that tried to break (yes!) Google's infrastructure (the stuff YouTube and Search run on) to make it stronger so it would never go down—not even during earthquakes or alien attacks! She now leads a team in Google Cloud that helps build infrastructure for Google and the world.

When Kripa was young, she changed what she wanted to be when she grew up every week! She loved math, science, the arts and Disney. She studied medicine, joined a band, ran a theater group, put on fashion shows and wrote books. Finally, her love for technology led her to Google. She still tries new things every day . . . and is currently exploring painting and fast cars!

Kripa's advice to young innovators: "Be curious and always ask questions—about everything! Be unafraid to try anything once."

Never stop being curious!

PARISA TABRIZ
INTREPID INNOVATOR

PARISA is an Engineering Director at Google who specializes in cybersecurity and the web. She is also called the *Security Princess* and *Browser Boss*. Have you ever used the Chrome browser? She leads the security team that keeps Chrome—the most popular browser in the world—safe from black-hat hackers!

Parisa became interested in cybersecurity when a website she built in college was hacked. In 2012, *Forbes* magazine named Parisa one of the top thirty tech pioneers under the age of thirty. While growing up, as the only girl in the family, Parisa had to either outmuscle or outsmart her two brothers. She also played lots of video games and outdoor sports with them.

Parisa's advice to young innovators: "I believe in optimizing for learning over success. You don't have to have everything figured out. Take the first step first!"

Take the first step first!

DIANE TANG
CODE COMMANDER

DIANE is a Google Fellow, and is sometimes also known as the *Queen of Clicks*. Diane designs systems and digs into data to ensure that we make good decisions. Have you used more than one Google product, like Search, Ads, Photos, Gmail . . . ? She leads teams that focus on data and analytics to understand how users use all Google products collectively rather than each individually!

Diane has never been afraid to tell people what she really thinks. In the third grade, she built a submarine for a science project. Her project report informed her teacher of the reasons why the project was not well-designed in the first place. Even today, she uses the same bluntness and honesty to drive projects forward.

Diane's advice to young innovators: "Always keep trying. Figuring it out is the fun part—and being frustrated often means you're just about to figure it out!"

Figuring it out is the fun part!

MARIAN CROAK
TENACIOUS TROUBLESHOOTER

MARIAN is a Vice President of Engineering at Google. She loves bringing new ideas and inventions to her work. Have you ever used the internet and wifi? She leads teams that design networks and services to bring the internet to the entire world! Marian owns over 125 patents and is honored in the Women in Technology International Hall of Fame.

Marian loved to perform experiments as a young girl with her chemistry set. Once, she almost set the house on fire! Her parents were very understanding but made sure she learned her lesson about asking for help when needed.

Marian's advice to young innovators: "At the end of every day, think about things that didn't go well. What can you do to make them better? Also, remember that you can't fix everything, so don't spend too much time worrying. Things *will* get better!"

Reflect on what you can improve!

GLOSSARY

< Algorithm > Step-by-step instructions for completing a task or solving a problem.

< Brainstorming > Collectively discussing thoughts to come up with ideas to solve a problem.

< Code or Program > A set of instructions for a computer, written in a programming language.

< Coding or Programming Languages > Languages used to communicate with a computer. Some examples include Java, C++, Python, Perl and Ruby.

< Computer > A machine that uses code to process information and perform calculations and operations.

< Computing Power > Elements of a computer that make large and difficult calculations possible, such as storage, memory and processors.

< Memory > The part of a computer that stores data short term.

< Processor > The "brain" of the computer that performs calculations.

< Storage > The part of a computer that stores data long term.

< Data Center > A large group of connected computers that store or process lots of data.

< Engineer > A general engineer invents, designs, builds and tests machines and systems. A software engineer (programmer) is an engineer who does all this by writing computer software.

< Googol > A giant number: 10 raised to the power of 100 (10^{100}), which is 1 followed by 100 zeroes.

< Troubleshooting > Problem solving to repair a broken machine or process.

The places mentioned in this story are inspired by GooglePlex (Google headquarters campus in California). *Innovation Plex*, *Data Center*, *Ideas Lab*, *Coding Pods* and *X-Space* illustrate locations where engineers build, play and innovate.

< with gratitude >

This book is made possible by the compassion of good people at Google. They stepped up in their personal capacities to help out in every avenue, to get this story of adventure and inclusion in the hands of fine young minds. THANK YOU to my fellow thinkers and tinkerers! Betsy Beyer and Isaac Andres for your incredible insights and prime patience with writing and reviewing. Amy Yip for your sweetly solid art direction. Leon Bayliss for boldly building the great website along with Brenda Fogg's generosity. Sara Heller for relentlessly relaying outreach opportunities along with Alana Beale and Wendy Manton. Misha Leder for diligently designing the fun activity sheets. Molly Moker for passionately producing the motivational videos. Marian Croak, Diane Tang, Kripa Krishnan and Parisa Tabriz for being superheroes inside and outside of the book and for instantly agreeing to share your inspiring stories. Steve Woods and Mohit Muthanna for perfectly propelling my enthusiasm. Google's diversity team for their kind support. To many other folks who helped out selflessly, and those who provided encouragement with virtual +1's and hallway kudos. Ipek Konak, our insanely talented illustrator, for weaving magic. The secret sauce publishing team of Page Two for making this complex project flow seamlessly: the editor, designer, proofreader, and strategists. Most importantly, my dearest family and friends, for being my champions and warriors, bringing comfort to every challenge, and somehow strangely loving me still.

< /with gratitude >